Acc 3900

LOOK AHEAD

a guide to working in...
Travel & Tourism

Deborah Fortune

www.heinemann.co.uk
Visit our website to find out more information about **Heinemann Library** books.

To order:
- ☎ Phone 44 (0) 1865 888066
- 📠 Send a fax to 44 (0) 1865 314091
- 💻 Visit the Heinemann Bookshop at www.heinemann.co.uk to browse our catalogue and order online.

First published in Great Britain by Heinemann Library, Halley Court, Jordan Hill, Oxford OX2 8EJ, a division of Reed Educational and Professional Publishing Ltd. Heinemann is a registered trademark of Reed Educational & Professional Publishing Limited.

OXFORD MELBOURNE AUCKLAND JOHANNESBURG BLANTYRE
GABORONE IBADAN PORTSMOUTH NH (USA) CHICAGO

© Reed Educational and Professional Publishing Ltd 2000
The moral right of the proprietor has been asserted.

All rights reserved. No part of this publication may be reproduced, stored in a retrieval system, or transmitted in any form or by any means, electronic, mechanical, photocopying, recording, or otherwise without either the prior written permission of the Publishers or a licence permitting restricted copying in the United Kingdom issued by the Copyright Licensing Agency Ltd, 90 Tottenham Court Road, London W1P 0LP.

Designed by Ambassador Litho Ltd
Originated by Ambassador Litho, Bristol
Printed in Hong Kong/China

ISBN 0 431 09482 9
04 03 02 01
10 9 8 7 6 5 4 3 2 1

British Library Cataloguing in Publication Data
Fortune, Deborah
    A guide to working in tourism and travel - (Look ahead)
    1.Tourist trade - Vocational guidance - Great Britain
    I. Title II.Tourism and travel
    338.4'791'02341

Acknowledgements
The Publishers would like to thank the following for permission to reproduce photographs: Adrian Meredith Photography, pp. 41, 44; Britain on View, p. 28; British Airways/Alan Meredith, p. 56; Crown Copyright: Historic Royal Palaces, p. 32; Greg Evans International Photo Library/Greg Balfour Evans, pp. 7, 42; Heinemann/David Townsend, pp. 35, 37, 54, pp. 19, 57/Trevor Clifford, John Walmsley, p. 16; Powerstock Zefa, pp. 39, 51; Spectrum Colour Library/L. Ball, p. 24; Tony stone Images, pp. 9/Doug Armand, 13/Bob Thomas, p. 47/Steward Cohen; World Pictures Feature-Pix Colour Library Ltd, pp. 20, 39.

Cover photograph reproduced with permission of Super Stock.

Our thanks to Joanna Dring, careers co-ordinator, Banbury School, Oxon for help in the preparation of this book.

Every effort has been made to contact copyright holders of any material reproduced in this book. Any omissions will be rectified in subsequent printings if notice is given to the Publisher.

Contents

Our shrinking world	4
Travel agents	10
Tour operators	16
Resort representatives	22
Tour managers	28
Tour guides	31
Tourist information centres	34
Airlines	39
Cruise ships and ferries	48
Getting into travel and tourism	52
Useful information, addresses & contacts	57
Get the jargon – a glossary of travel and tourism terms	62
Index	64

Technical words, jargon and specialist terms are explained in the glossary.

Our shrinking world

It is true that the world really is getting smaller. Journeys that once took days and days now last only a matter of hours, and even the most remote, far-flung places in the world have opened up to mass tourism.

⭐ You can fly to almost any part of the inhabited world. This map shows just some of the places you can fly to from the UK.

TRAVEL & TOURISM

The travel and tourism industry is one of the fastest growing and most important areas of employment in the world. It is said to be the world's largest industry, generating more than 10 per cent of global income. It is also estimated that by the year 2006 there will be 385 million jobs worldwide that are directly related to travel and tourism. At present somewhere in the world, one new job is created in the industry every 2.4 seconds!

> **CONSIDER THIS...**
> ECONOMISTS HAVE SAID THAT THE 21ST CENTURY ECONOMY WILL BE DRIVEN BY THREE 'SUPER-SERVICES':
> ● COMMUNICATIONS
> ● INFORMATION TECHNOLOGY
> ● TRAVEL AND TOURISM.

Why? Well, the population as a whole has more leisure time and more money to spend than in any other period of history, and increasingly we are choosing to spend that leisure time on holidays and travel. Add that to the fact that more and more people are taking more than one holiday a year, and you get an idea of where all this growth is coming from.

Here, there and everywhere

At some stage in our lives we all become customers of the travel and tourism industry. For example, we might:
- fly to America
- go on a cruise
- catch a train to visit some relatives
- go on a coach tour around the Pennines
- go on a holiday to Majorca
- visit the Natural History Museum
- take a guided tour of Edinburgh
- visit Alton Towers
- take a car ferry to France.

All of these activities and more are part of the world of travel and tourism. Throughout our lives, whether for business or pleasure, we are consumers of the services provided by the industry. Travel is becoming increasingly important in a shrinking world where many people have more time and expendable finance than they have ever had before.

Is it all glamour and fun?

Because nearly every one of us has had contact with people who work in this industry, we often think that we know what it would be like to do this sort of work ourselves:

'I went on a package holiday to Spain and we had a really nice courier at the hotel. She told us all about the place and arranged some coach trips for us. That's the sort of job I'd like.'

Glossy holiday brochures and television soaps can give the impression that working in travel and tourism is simply a fun, glamorous career and a great way to see the rest of the world.

Is this true? Well, in part it is, but this is only one small part of a much more complicated picture. Obviously there are opportunities to travel in some jobs within the industry, but there are many more jobs where most of the work is carried out in offices. In such a large and complex industry where millions of people are employed offering a variety of services to the public it is difficult to generalize about working practices. But there are some common themes in certain jobs that can give us a feel for what that type of work is like. And there is one common factor throughout the industry – the customer!

In the travel and tourism industry the most important person is the customer. The aim is to ensure that all customers feel comfortable and that they have everything they need to fully enjoy their stay. An enormous amount of work goes on behind the scenes to ensure that this happens. As customers, we see the public face of travel and tourism, but what is it really like to work as a resort representative or as a travel agent?

What is it like to fly as a member of an air cabin crew or to work on a cruise ship?

The true story may not be exactly as you imagine. For example, did you know that most holiday couriers are only employed for six months of the year? Did you know that working as a flight attendant on long-haul flights where you have to fly between time zones can alter your body clock so that, for example, your body wants to go to sleep in the middle of the afternoon and get up at midnight?

There is a lot more to the travel and tourism industry than you think!

⭐ *Airline staff offer willing assistance to passengers with children and pushchairs.*

What sort of person do you need to be to work in such a huge and varied industry?

Obviously there are many different jobs, needing all sorts of different skills. The flight attendant and the travel agent both require training in very specific and different areas but, as is the case for the majority of jobs in the tourism and travel industry, the work they both do will only be enjoyed by those who like work that involves dealing with people.

Pay levels are not high for many jobs in the industry, but then people do not usually go into travel and tourism solely for the money. Many jobs in the industry are demanding, but they are likely to offer variety and, if not the chance to travel as part of the job, then at least the opportunity for discounted travel through their employer.

For example, only a tiny proportion of airline employees actually fly. Many more are employed in **customer services** and **operations** on the ground, but they all get discounted flights. That can mean paying only 10 per cent of a full fare, which would make a weekend shopping trip to New York almost as cheap as a trip to the high street!

Any job where you spend most of your time dealing with the public can be challenging. People expect the best when they go on holiday, and if their standards are not met they will look for someone to blame. The resort rep, the airline staff, the tour operator, the travel agent all, at some time, have to take a tongue lashing and smile nicely in return. This is often the hardest part of the job, but it has to be done. Of course, there is also the possibility of satisfaction when a customer says, 'Thank you very much for sorting that out.'

⭐ *The tour guide has taken his group to a viewpoint overlooking English Harbour, Antigua in the Caribbean.*

Holidays to go!

The package holiday has revolutionized people's attitude to travel. Areas like Mexico, Cuba and the South Sea Islands, which had previously only been available to a privileged few, are now offered in brochures alongside more traditional resorts in Spain and Greece. This trend looks set to grow. Much of the continent of Africa is looking to develop its tourist potential and the opening up of mainland China has yet to be fully exploited. One of the biggest growth areas is in world travel – package holidays on a grand scale offering customers an organized trip around the world. These are becoming more and more affordable for many people. Specialized packages catering for anything from walking in the foothills of the Himalayas to whale watching in Alaska are another recent development. The industry is constantly investigating new opportunities to attract new customers.

The ease of air travel has obviously had an enormous effect on the spectacular growth of the travel and tourism industry. But transport is only one area of the industry. Hotels, self-catering accommodation, tours, entertainment and leisure facilities, financial services and insurance are all part of the overall package. All these create work for some of the millions of people employed in this fast moving, varied industry.

Travel agents

Look along most of the high streets in our towns and you will come across at least one travel agency. There are over 2000 travel agencies in the UK, with almost 7000 offices across the country. These agencies vary from the small, independent, one-person firms to the large international companies employing thousands of staff.

There are two main types of travel agency. The first is independent travel agencies which handle holidays from many different companies. The second is agencies that are owned by one single company. The main purpose of these agencies is to promote their own holidays.

Whatever the size of the agency the job they perform is similar.

The **travel agent's** role within the travel and tourism industry is to provide a link between the public and the holiday industry. It is their job to inform the customer about what is available. This might be package holidays, where all the component parts of a holiday – travel, accommodation, meals, etc – are offered within one total price. It could also be something more specific, for example:

- a short break in the UK
- ferry or air travel
- traveller's cheques and other foreign currency needs
- around-the-world travel
- explanation of the inoculations that are necessary when visiting certain exotic countries.

All of these services are offered through a travel agency. The good travel agent will have knowledge of all these areas and more.

On top of all this product knowledge they also need to develop an expertise with the different computer systems that are used for accessing information, for making travel bookings and for arranging accommodation.

There are now computer systems within most travel agencies that can match an individual customer's needs as closely as possible with a complete holiday package – travel, accommodation, insurance – and a holiday destination.

With increased use of the Internet to access information on travel and accommodation, it is even more important that the travel agent can offer more than just information on what is available, where and what it might cost. The successful agent must offer the customer advice and guidance that they cannot get elsewhere. This means that staff must be well trained in both the product knowledge that they need to match the customer's requirements and the high level of service expected by the customer.

In return for the sales that the travel agent makes, they receive a payment or commission from the company offering the services. This could be a tour operator, an airline, a ferry company or a coach service.

Some travel agencies offer extra services, such as insurance or the provision of foreign currency, for which they also receive commission.

Because travel agencies are part of a fast growing industry, as is the case within other areas of retailing, there are often opportunities for enthusiastic travel advisers to move into management at a fairly quick rate.

A REAL ALL-ROUNDER

A TRAVEL AGENT MUST POSSESS A COMBINATION OF SKILLS. THEY MUST BE GOOD AT DEALING WITH THE PUBLIC AND AT SELLING PACKAGES AND SERVICES. THEY MUST ALSO HAVE THE ORGANIZATIONAL AND IT SKILLS TO MANAGE THE COMPLICATED SYSTEMS INVOLVED WITH SEARCHING FOR AND TICKETING AND BOOKING HOLIDAYS.

ON TOP OF ALL THIS IT IS IMPORTANT FOR THE TRAVEL AGENT TO FEEL CONFIDENT IN HANDLING THE FINANCIAL SIDE OF BOOKINGS AND PAYMENT. SO NUMERACY SKILLS ARE ALSO NEEDED.

IN OTHER WORDS, IT HELPS TO BE A *REAL ALL-ROUNDER*!

Anna – Travel Adviser

Anna Mackay works in a busy high street travel agency that is part of a national chain.

While I was in my final year at school I did a week's work experience in a travel agent and decided that was what I wanted to do. I applied for a GNVQ Leisure and Tourism course at the local college, which would have given me a useful background to the work, but then a vacancy for a trainee came up in another agency. The job meant that I could work towards my NVQ2 through the Travel Training Company.

A typical day varies depending on the time of year. January is usually the busiest time, when we open the branch on Sundays to cope with the demand from people wanting to book their summer holidays. The day usually starts with a meeting for all the staff before the shop opens at 9.00 am. This is when we are told about any new special promotions or changes that might affect the day's sales.

Everyone in the branch works on Saturdays and we take a day off in the week. It's part of my job to make sure that there aren't any empty spaces in the brochure display. I also help with the display of posters, which we have in the shop area and in the window and change regularly to catch the customer's eye.

When I first came into the job I learnt a lot about dealing with customers by sitting with one of the experienced advisers and seeing how it was done. I can now book customers through our computer system and help them match their requirements through talking with them and then searching through what is available.

I had a six month induction period when I was trained on the computer systems and also went on a number of company training courses to learn about customer service and selling skills. And I am now working for my NVQ2 in Travel. My progress is checked by my manager and an assessor from the Travel Training Company.

It is quite a responsibility taking deposits, especially when people are sometimes spending thousands on their holidays! So we often spend a long time dealing with just one client and this can mean phoning them at home to confirm bookings and pass on any extra information they might need. We also tell customers about the other services that we offer like holiday insurance and currency.

When I started as a trainee I was getting about £5000 per year but that figure has already risen and as I get more experience and more sales I can earn more money! At present I am on almost £12,000 and can earn more with commission.

There are downsides to every job and I do find the pressure to get it right all the time can be difficult. You can't afford to make mistakes when you are dealing with other people's money.

But generally I like the fact that every day is different in this job. I really enjoy the busy atmosphere of the agency and it helps that I like dealing with all sorts of people and am interested in travel.

You never know who is going to walk through the door next or where they'll want to go!

⭐ The travel agent is helping her customers decide on their holiday plans.

Business travel

There is an increasing number of travel agencies that deal with specialist markets. Business travel is a growth area as the business world becomes more and more global, and there is money to be made booking business travellers into first or business class travel.

There are pressures in this type of work different from those of high street travel agency work.

Bookings often have to be made at short notice and regular business clients expect a different type of service – speed and convenience are often more important than choice and value for money. It is especially important for agents to be confident and have extremely good inter-personal skills.

As mentioned earlier, the growth of the Internet is likely to have an increasing effect on the development of travel agencies in the future. In the last few years more people have been making their own travel and accommodation arrangements through the world wide web and this trend looks likely to expand. In response to this, some travel agencies have recently been established that only operate through the Internet. We do not know how these developments may effect the future of the high street travel agency, although it is likely that with increasing travel and leisure time many customers will still find the need for someone with specialist knowledge to help coordinate their plans. At present over 90 per cent of package holiday deals are sold through high street travel agencies and tour operators.

What makes a good travel agent?

You never know who is going to walk through the door, so you must be someone who enjoys the challenge of variety and 'thinking on your feet'. It is also a job where you are always busy. There is always something that needs doing and very few quiet periods.

You should enjoy using information technology. The impact of IT on the work of the travel agent cannot be overstressed. It is immediately obvious when you walk into any high street agency that a lot of time is spent at a screen retrieving information. This aspect of the work will become even more important, but of course you must also have the ability to work with the public.

It helps to have a good sense of and interest in the geography of the world. With long haul and exotic travel becoming more common, it is important for a travel agent to be able to communicate to customers some knowledge of their destination, including things like climate, local geography and culture. A liking for travel is also important. It helps to have an enthusiasm for the work and so be able to pass that enthusiasm on to the customer.

You must be efficient and self-confident in all your dealings with both customers and tour operators. Above all, you should be someone who likes dealing with people.

It is possible to get into travel agency work straight from school after GCSEs or after one or two years in further education. A well-recognized and structured training programme is in place for young people, leading to NVQs through the Travel Training Company. (See *'Getting into travel and tourism'* on page 52.)

The Travel Training Company is one of the industry's most important training organizations. It offers a wide range of training packages to people entering the industry and helps to develop and promote training opportunities in travel and tourism.

Tour operators

A **tour operator** is a company offering a complete range of holiday services to their customers. Services such as transport to and from destinations, accommodation and insurance are all offered in one package for a single price – hence the term 'package holidays'.

The presence of **resort representatives** or **tour guides** who work for the company's customers at the actual holiday site is something that is often included within the package deal.

✪ *Tour operators organize complete holiday packages including transport, accommodation and insurance.*

The idea of the package holiday is to bring together the various elements of a holiday and offer a complete 'deal' to customers, who may find it difficult or inconvenient – through pressure of time or lack of knowledge – to arrange all the elements themselves. The simplicity and convenience of a package holiday have opened up foreign travel to a wider market and greatly increased the numbers of customers taking holidays.

Some tour operators are large companies employing hundreds of people while others are one- or two-person operations. Often tour operators advertise their holidays through glossy brochures with attractive photos and text designed to appeal to customers. The design and production of these brochures is part of the tour operator's work.

There is a growing number of tour operators who offer specialist holidays to customers. These can include round-the-world, activity and adventure holidays as well as other types of holiday.

Some operators specialize in a narrow range, offering and promoting only a certain type of holiday. For example, recent years have seen the growth of holidays in the UK offered by centres with covered leisure areas, such as Center Parcs. These centres offer:
- accommodation
- organized sports and leisure time
- catering
- entertainment
- special facilities for, and supervision of, children

all in one package and for a single price.

Other tour operators offer a complete range of holidays to choose from.

Some of the larger companies even run their own travel agencies to promote their products, while others advertise and sell direct to the public or through independent agencies.

There is a whole range of jobs associated with the large companies that offer holiday products. Like any large business, these companies employ people in administration, sales, finance and information technology. Outlined below are some of the more specialist jobs, which have a more direct link to the travel and tourism industry.

Reservations People working in reservations have most of their contact with the public over the phone. They take enquiries and check availability and details before processing bookings. They could be dealing with holiday bookings from travel agents working on behalf of customers or through talking to customers directly. They have to work calmly and carefully to ensure that bookings are accurate and often have to be able to give advice on booking procedures or brochure details as they work. This is mainly a clerical role using computerized systems. However, in many companies it is possible to progress from here to other roles. Team-work and good communication skills are most important and specifically a good telephone manner.

Customer services This is often the initial point of contact for potential customers and is therefore a very important role for the tour operator. Those working in customer services have to have a broad knowledge of all the services that the company offers or to know to whom they should refer customers if necessary. A good telephone manner is essential as most customer contact is by phone. Team-work and good communication skills are important. Again, this is mainly a clerical job using computerized systems and although it is helpful to have an interest in travel and tourism, it is not essential.

Marketing This is a very important area for the tour operator. The marketing department is the part of the company that researches where people might want to go and how to tell them what the tour operator is offering. Within marketing there will be work looking at future developments, advertising, and producing brochures. Large companies have separate departments working in each of these areas. Smaller tour operators may employ only a few people who each cover a range of areas.

Sales There will also be sales staff whose job it is to promote and sell the company's products to travel agencies. This work might include hosting promotional events and training travel agency staff about new products. In a large company that could be an enormous task, handling several millions of brochures each season.

⭐ *There are brochures for almost every kind of holiday.*

Sally – Tour Contractor

Sally Smyth works for a specialist tour operator who deals mainly in winter/ski holidays.

Between school and college I took a year out and part of that time I worked as a chalet maid in a ski resort in the Swiss Alps. It was hard work but was good for my French and my skiing, although I didn't get to ski as much as I'd hoped. After my degree in Business Studies I looked around for a job that might offer some travel.

I now work as one of a small team within the contracts department and it is our job to sort out the contract arrangements with the hotels and the airlines that accommodate our customers. We also deal with all the other services like ski schools and passes and coach companies. Contracts have to be sorted out months before the season starts, and this involves travelling to the resorts to meet with local hoteliers and other people to finalize details and make sure that our customers are being offered the level of service that we expect for them.

Working for the company means that I do get a good discount on any personal travel and ski holidays, but most of my work is carried out back at the office working nine to five most days. I earn £22,000 per year plus a share in the company bonus scheme.

I enjoy being able to use the skills I studied for. Negotiating contracts is very satisfying and it's good to use my French. It can be frustrating when external circumstances affect our arrangements. In our case that usually means the weather! And there's nothing we can do about that!

⭐ Ski holiday packages can include ski schools and passes as well as transport and accommodation.

What makes a good tour operator?

DOMESTIC TOUR OPERATORS ARRANGE PACKAGE HOLIDAYS WITHIN THE UK.

OUTBOUND TOUR OPERATORS ARRANGE PACKAGE HOLIDAYS FROM THE UK TO OTHER COUNTRIES.

INBOUND TOUR OPERATORS OFFER PACKAGE HOLIDAYS FOR PEOPLE COMING TO THE UK.

To be a good tour operator you need to be someone who enjoys dealing with the public, although a lot of your contact with people may be over the phone or increasingly through the Internet, rather than face to face. Customer relations are essential to the industry and the customer is seen as the most important element of any package holiday.

IT skills are once again very important in this job as this aspect of travel and tourism operations is predominantly computer-based. It helps to have a good understanding of the travel industry as a whole, as you may have to deal with people in different sections of the business. The work of people employed in tour operations is wide ranging so, to be successful, it helps to have an overview of how all the parts of tour operations fit together. As much of the work is really administrative, an interest and understanding of office skills and business systems is essential.

Training in the industry varies from job to job depending on the working environment and needs of the company or department you are working in. Much of the administrative and commercial business of tour operators relies on the customer relations and business skills of their staff. Staff often have business qualifications or work towards NVQs whilst in work. Marketing and sales staff have specialized training and qualifications to suit their area of work and others such as photographers and copywriters are self-employed and are contracted in for specific work. Other staff working directly with holidaymakers at resorts are often on short-term contracts, receive most of their training on the job and at present do not tend to follow any structured training.

Resort representatives

The role of the **resort representative** (usually called the 'rep') or **courier** is to look after, or 'represent', a tour operator's customers while they are staying at a holiday site either in the UK or abroad.

The rep's first contact with customers may be when they meet them at the airport or on arrival at their site or accommodation. However, their work for that customer will have started long before that point. It is usually the courier's job to allocate accommodation to customers, taking into account any particular requests individuals may have made when they booked, for example:
- family rooms
- wheel chair access
- vegetarian meals.

Reps have to meet clients on their arrival and, if necessary, arrange transport from the airport or other arrival point to their accommodation. They also need to be prepared to act as an informal guide, providing information on what facilities are available in the area and sometimes promoting any excursions that are organized by the tour operator.

The rep acts as the link between the holidaymakers and all the holiday services that their customers expect during their stay. They may need to liaise with many different people, from staff in hotels and holiday complexes through air, train and coach companies to local tour guides and shopkeepers.

Essentially being a resort rep means that when you are on duty you are available to your clients 24 hours a day, sorting out any of their problems – large or small.

Couriers have to be available at all times to help clients with any problems or queries they may have and be prepared to step in when necessary. This could mean helping with anything from advising on local restaurants to dealing with lost passports, traffic accidents or major illnesses.

As well as dealing with the queries of clients, it is also usually the rep's responsibility to complete any paperwork and accounts that the tour operator needs.

The job requires a great deal of flexibility and self-reliance. Customer needs will vary from client to client and the day-to-day duties of a courier can be numerous and varied. Usually reps are on call for 24 hours of the day although they often have some free time each day when they are 'off duty'. However, if a problem arises with a client they usually have to respond without delay.

Reps normally spend a whole season at a resort, although they need to be flexible about where they are based and may have to move at short notice as directed by their employer.

Summer holiday reps tend to be employed on-site between April and October, although some may work only from June to September. Winter reps tend to work from December to April. Some reps will move from winter to summer contracts but find themselves unemployed in the early winter months. All reps work on short-term contracts and most have to reapply year after year, so there is little job security.

Tour operators usually recruit people in their early twenties, although children's reps may be employed at eighteen or nineteen years of age if they are suitably qualified.

Children's reps

There are possibilities for specializing as a resort rep if you want to.

Children's reps can work exclusively with children, setting up entertainment for a whole range of different age groups from toddlers through to teenagers. This could also include arranging childminding or supervising meal times. Or even dressing up in costume to promote the tour operator's services!

Some companies will expect their children's reps to have recognized childcare or teaching qualifications, while others look for experience of working with children.

There are also opportunities for those who have a level of skill in a sport like canoeing or in an outdoor pursuit like rock climbing or bird watching, to specialize in coaching or leading group activities. Again, required qualifications vary from company to company.

⭐ *Canoeing instruction is popular with adults as well as children.*

There is little set training for resort reps. Most employers offer an initial few days' training either in the UK or at the resort itself. Many will supply training manuals and offer experienced staff to help deal with particular problems but there is little overall structured training offered.

Vacancies for resort work do not tend to be advertised but positions may be offered to people who have applied directly to the company on what is called a speculative application. Competition for vacancies can be intense. Pay for this type of work varies from company to company and can be anything from around £80 per week to £145 depending on the responsibilities of the post. Reps receive free accommodation and insurance cover while working and are often provided with a uniform, which they are usually expected to wear during working hours.

Working in a holiday resort in the UK offers a different experience from that of the tour rep abroad. Jobs are offered in a number of areas, the most competitive being customer operations, which includes entertainment staff. There is a minimum age of eighteen years for employment. Staff are employed for the summer season and must be prepared to work long hours. Entertainment staff must offer performance ability to a high standard.

What makes a good resort representative?

You need to be adaptable and have a flexible approach to the work you may have to undertake. Experience of dealing with the public is helpful. Being confident and self-reliant is essential. Communication skills are important and if you have at least conversational ability in a second language, it is a definite asset.

Paul – Holiday Courier

Paul Foster works as a courier for a camping company that operates in Europe.

This is my first job since leaving university. My ambition is to join the police force. I took the job because I was told that I needed some experience working with the public and I fancied some time living and working abroad.

I signed on for a full season, which is actually only six months. It is possible to work a half season, three months, but you tend to get better placements if the company thinks you'll be around for a while, and I do want the experience.

I didn't get a lot of training before I came to the site, but there is a very comprehensive training manual that all the couriers are given and that covers most things that you'll need to know. They also tend to put two couriers together on the bigger sites so that you can help each other out. If you are on a smaller one you could be on your own but there should be a supervisor not too far away to help when needed. Mind you, our supervisor covers the whole of southern France and northern Spain, so it's best if you can work out the problem yourself!

My job is to prepare the tents for people and clean them out at the end of their stay. I also welcome holidaymakers to the site, show them around and explain all the facilities. We run a children's club twice a week for our clients and it's part of my job to organize treasure hunts and things to entertain the kids.

I am tied to the campsite most of the time. Clients are always telling me about places they have visited, which is useful to pass on to other clients but I don't get much time to see them for myself.

The company provides all couriers with a uniform and a bike for getting around the site. We get about £60 per week, which isn't much for the hours that we work, but there's no accommodation to pay for. We also get a bonus if we complete a whole season and get paid extra for clearing tents on sites at the end of the season.

It helps to be a good organizer and to be fairly self-reliant. I have to turn my hand to all sorts of things from cleaning to mending fridges.

Some clients can be really awkward, constantly calling me to their tents with complaints and queries, but you have to smile and go along with it all. Most are great, though, and just get on with enjoying themselves, and if I happen to drop by around suppertime there is often an invitation to stay and have a beer!

It's a great way to get the experience I need, and a suntan!

Holiday couriers are responsible for organizing activities for children.

Tour managers

The **tour manager's** job is to oversee the smooth running of a holiday that involves a group of clients travelling from site to site. To do this they generally travel with their clients throughout the tour. They are employed by a tour operator and are there to ensure that all the aspects of a tour, from travel arrangements to accommodation, are of an acceptable standard for their clients. It is up to the tour manager to outline all aspects of the holiday to the group at the beginning of the tour and to deal with any problems that may arise along the way. They usually give background information to places visited, liaise with hotel staff, arrange comfort stops as necessary, deal with any border controls and generally look after the welfare of the customers.

Louis – Administrator and Tour Manager

Louis Muldive works for a coach company, which offers European tours.

I suppose I really have two jobs. During most of the year I work at our head office doing mainly administrative stuff like taking bookings, confirming hotels, ferry bookings etc. – mainly dealing with clients as they arrange their holidays. Then in the spring and summer season, which is when most of our business takes place, I lead some of the coach tours.

When I am based in the office I get paid a set wage, about £18,000 per year, and when I am out on tour with groups the company pays me an extra bonus for the longer hours that I work.

We are a family firm so people here are used to having a number of different roles. And I enjoy the variety of the two different types of work.

I came into tourism because I wanted to use my languages – I did an HND in Business and French – and because I enjoy dealing with people. Many of our clients are in their later years. They often have specific concerns about the trip. Often it's the food or the travelling times that concern them. I have to take all these into account. It is up to me to gauge the mood of the customers and make sure that everything runs smoothly throughout the trip. I sort out any problems with accommodation and arrange any special trips we offer.

It can be really hard work, especially having to be bright and jolly when you have a stinking headache and are seeing something for the tenth time! All in all, though, I enjoy the job.

I like dealing with people and it is really satisfying when you are told what a great holiday you have helped them to have.

⭐ Tour managers like Louis spend much of the year in the office arranging holidays for people. But he also enjoys conducting coach tours for his company in the busy spring and summer seasons.

Tour managers need to be good organizers and be able to cope with all sorts of unseen events. When working, like the **resort representative**, the tour manager is never really off duty. They live and travel with their group throughout the tour and so are in very close contact. They must be available to their clients whenever they need them. It can be hard work.

It helps to have a working knowledge of one or more foreign languages and to have an interest in and understanding of the customs and culture of the area.

Tour managers tend not to be employed until their early twenties and most have had experience of dealing with the public. Employment tends to be seasonal and most tour operators pay their tour managers a daily rate and include free accommodation and expenses.

> **CONSIDER THIS…**
>
> THE TOUR MANAGER MUST WORK CLOSELY WITH GROUPS OF TOURISTS. THEREFORE THE ABILITY TO GET ON WITH ALL SORTS OF DIFFERENT PEOPLE IS VERY IMPORTANT.
>
> A TOUR COULD BE ANYTHING FROM TWO OR THREE DAYS TO A MONTH OR EVEN LONGER. MOST ACCOMPANY GROUPS ABROAD ON FOREIGN TRIPS, BUT SOME ARE EMPLOYED TO TRAVEL WITH INCOMING TOURISTS IN THIS COUNTRY.

What makes a good tour manager?

Like the resort rep, it helps to be self-confident and self-reliant. An ability to communicate and work well with the public is essential. It is also an advantage to have at least a conversational ability in a second language. Patience and adaptability are of great importance.

Tour guides

A **tour guide** is someone who specializes in showing visitors around a particular location. It could be:
- a city
- a town
- a country area
- a stately home
- a castle
- even an abandoned mine.

The increase in tourism within the UK has led to the development of many different opportunities for this type of work.

Tour guides may be employed by tour managers to take visitors through a part of their holiday or they may be employed by private establishments such as galleries, museums or castles or by national organizations, such as national parks or heritage centres.

Like a lot of jobs within the industry, tour guide positions are offered on a seasonal basis, although in places like London, the season is becoming extended as tourism becomes more of a year-round pursuit. Many guides are self-employed and work on a contract basis. Those who work in permanent jobs for organizations may take on other roles during quieter periods of the year. Some establishments rely on willing volunteers to act as guides.

Regional tourist boards run training courses for tour guides, which can lead to a badge qualification. Competition for training can be fierce with most places going to people aged 25 and older who have good local knowledge and often relevant experience of dealing with people.

What makes a good tour guide?

Although it is important to have an interest in and a basic knowledge of an area it is once again more important for a guide to have good communication skills and the ability to relate to a wide range of people.

When recruiting tour guides, personality and attitude are most important. And although a lot of guides get into the work because they have a personal interest in the area, much of the background knowledge is gained in training.

⭐ *Costumed guides like these at Hampton Court help to give tourists a sense of the history behind the famous palace where they work.*

John – Tour Guide

John Robbins works as a tour guide in a Tudor manor house that is open to the public and is run as a registered charity.

The manor house is a very popular tourist attraction in the area and we get people visiting from all around the world. It helps to have a real interest in history; I researched a lot of the information that I pass on to the visitors myself. But you also have to be able to talk to all sorts of people. Some of our visitors have no real knowledge of British history so it helps if you can put yourself in their shoes and explain what they are seeing in a way that will help them to understand it.

I work when they need me, which is on average about three days a week during the summer season and less over the winter when we only open for organized group visits.

As well as showing people around the house and telling them about its history I am involved in the special event days that we put on. When we are doing re-enactments I dress up in Tudor clothes and act the part of a Tudor lord. All the staff join in and we try to make the house come alive, as it would have been all those years ago.

You have to be a bit of an actor and really throw yourself into the part as well as remembering the historical details. I particularly enjoy the school parties that come around, and try to get the children involved as much as possible.

It's not a well-paid job – when I am working I get about £80 per week – but I love the work and get a real pleasure in helping visitors appreciate what a fascinating place they are experiencing.

Tourist information centres

The main aim of the tourist information centres (TICs) scattered across the country is to encourage visitors to spend as much time and money in their particular area as possible. In 1998 over 24 million overseas visitors came to the UK spending over £8 billion in tourism-related areas.

Individual centres vary according to setting and size but there are tasks common to them all. Some share premises with museums and libraries while others have purpose-built premises.

A **tourist information assistant's** job is to deal with all queries that come into the centre. These could be by phone or e-mail, letter or fax, or through personal callers who come into the centre.

A lot of information specific to local and national tourist sites is held in most centres and bookings can often be made for local museums, galleries, tours and sporting events. However, most centres provide an even wider service offering travel and accommodation advice as well as holding up-to-date lists of theatres and concert halls, current events and attractions.

Tourist information centres not only deal with foreign tourists, but also help British visitors and locals wanting news on events in the area. Many TICs pride themselves on representing their communities and take great delight in arranging special events and promotions to attract visitors.

> **CONSIDER THIS...**
>
> THERE ARE FOUR NATIONAL AND ELEVEN REGIONAL TOURIST BOARDS IN THE UK WHOSE ROLE IS TO PROMOTE TOURISM IN THIS COUNTRY.
>
> WITH FOREIGN VISITORS BRINGING OVER £8 BILLION INTO THE UK EACH YEAR, EMPLOYMENT WITHIN THE TOURIST BOARDS IS GROWING AND IS LIKELY TO RISE IN THE FUTURE.
>
> ROLES EXIST IN MARKETING, PUBLICITY AND PROMOTIONS AND EVENT ORGANIZATION.

The range of questions that are asked is huge, for example:
- Where can I catch a bus, train?
- Can you tell me what is on at the local theatres and cinemas?
- Is there accommodation available locally?

The tourist centre assistant has to be prepared to find answers to all of these queries and more.

Some centres write their own tourist books and leaflets for local places of interest and all handle a huge range of promotional material. Most centres also run an accommodation booking service for visitors.

Many centres sell books and guides, some sell souvenirs of local interest and it is often the job of the assistants to reorder and update goods.

⭐ *Tourist information centres help visitors to get the best from their stay in the area.*

Savi – Tourist Information Centre Assistant

Savi Bhatti works in a busy Tourist Information Centre in Stratford upon Avon, a very popular tourist town. She earns £17,000 per annum.

Working in tourist information means you have to be prepared for anything. No two days are ever the same, but that suits me just fine, because I enjoy the variety of the job. Before the doors open at the start of each day we make sure that all the literature we offer to our visitors is stocked up.

The tourist season here is really all year round, we are one of the places that visitors feel they must visit when they come to the UK, so the pace is always pretty hectic.

As people come from all over the world it obviously helps if you have another language, but we deal with so many different nationalities that I spend a lot of my time using sign language or drawing diagrams for people.

We do a lot of bookings for various attractions and people often ask us to recommend hotels and places to stay.

Lots of tourist buses run from outside the centre. We don't operate the tours ourselves but you still find yourself being questioned about when, where and how much. It's all part of the job!

It's the same with lots of our queries. There are times when you might not know the answer yourself, so it's important to know where to look and who to ask. Some of the questions you get asked seem so strange. For example, 'Do you have any photographs of Shakespeare?' and some tourists can be quite rude and very demanding.

But then you have to remember that to some of our visitors we are just one stop on a world tour and they feel pressured to make the most of their stay. Still, it's hard to keep smiling sometimes.

Not all our visitors are from abroad. We get a lot of people on weekend breaks and locals pop in to ask about events in the area.

When I was in school I didn't really know what I wanted to do, but I did think that I would like a job dealing with people. The GNVQ in Leisure and Tourism seemed like a good idea and I enjoyed the course. After that I got a job working in a hotel and enjoyed that, but after a while found that working evening shifts interfered with my social life.

We run a rota system here and although it means working Saturdays and a couple of late evenings in the summer it's okay. I was lucky to get this job. I think that my time working in the hotel reception really helped. I feel a pride in living in such a beautiful place and enjoy telling people about my home town.

⭐ *Tourist Information Centre assistants need to know practically everything about their area, including the bus times!*

Most of the work of the tourist centre assistant is carried out across the counter with the public, dealing with the wide range of queries that relate to local tourism. Telephone and, increasingly, Internet queries are also an important point of contact. There are, however, times when the TIC assistant may be asked to conduct special visitors personally. The variety of this type of work means that it is helpful to have a flexible attitude to what might become part of your job. It also means that the job of a TIC assistant will have many differences from area to area. Of course, there are routine parts of the work that remain constant – the understanding of local facilities and the operation of an accommodation booking service are required nationwide, as is ensuring the supply of accurate up-to-date information for visitors.

What makes a good tourist centre assistant?

To be a successful tourist centre assistant you need extremely good communication skills and to be able to handle a wide variety of people. An outgoing, friendly personality is essential. You also need to be fairly patient and able to keep cool under pressure as once again a job advising the public can be fairly testing. A working knowledge of a foreign language is useful, if not essential, in some popular areas like London.

Obviously it helps to have good local knowledge and an interest in what is going on!

Large centres with all-year-round tourism may employ several full-time staff who work as a team. Many smaller centres operate with part-time or seasonal staff.

Airlines

So far, the jobs we have concentrated on have been in tourism. We will now look at some relevant job opportunities in the travel industry. First, in this chapter we will look at working for airlines, and in the next chapter we will look at cruise ship opportunities.

Airlines are huge businesses often employing many thousands of people in a whole range of jobs from cleaners to accountants. Although all of these jobs are important in the smooth running of the business, we are going to concentrate on those roles that are most associated with a direct interest in travel and tourism.

⭐ *Far-away places with strange-sounding names – these are some of the ways to get there and enjoy them!*

TRAVEL & TOURISM

Flight attendant/ air steward/stewardess

> **CONSIDER THIS...**
> THE TERM 'WAITER OR WAITRESS IN THE SKY' HAS SOMETIMES BEEN APPLIED TO THE WORK OF FLIGHT ATTENDANTS. ALTHOUGH THIS IS AN OVER-SIMPLIFICATION AND THERE ARE OBVIOUS DIFFERENCES BETWEEN THE TWO JOBS, SUCH AS THE RESPONSIBILITY FOR PASSENGER SAFETY AND THE CHANCE FOR TRAVEL, THE REALITY IS THAT A LARGE PART OF THE TIME IN THE AIR IS SPENT WAITING ON PASSENGERS.

The first role for anyone working as a **flight attendant** or **air steward/stewardess** must be to ensure the safety and well-being of their passengers.

The image of those working on board aircraft can be pretty glamorous on the surface. The picture of the flight attendant gliding up and down luxurious 747s calm and smiling, offering the occasional glass of wine or tray of food and later to smile the passengers off the flight with a cheery 'Thank you for travelling with us!' can be misleading.

In reality, staff will have started work at least an hour before the passengers arrive, checking that vital safety equipment is in order, that each passenger has the correct safety notices and that the plane is tidy. It is the responsibility of the attendants to check that there is the correct number of in-flight meals and drinks and that the serving carts are full and the food trays complete.

With their smiles in place, once the flight is loading, attendants check tickets and welcome passengers on board.

All flights begin with the demonstration of safety procedures and equipment and when all passengers are secured it is the attendant who lets the pilot know when they are ready for take-off.

On short-haul flights the staff may have less than an hour to feed and 'process' a plane full of people.

⭐ *Flight attendants serve in-flight meals to passengers.*

The working conditions in the plane's galleys are often cramped and attendants often have little or no time to see any of the exotic destinations they may be flying to as they have to rest and prepare for return flights in a matter of hours. They also have to be prepared to work unsocial hours, covering night and weekend flights, which can interfere with a personal life. However, working for an airline usually means greatly subsidized air travel, and good rates of pay are often supplemented by allowances for unsociable hours and extensive overseas work.

Because of the glamorous image and generous pay and perks of this work, there is incredible competition for jobs, with some airlines receiving over 25,000 open enquiries each year. But if you like dealing with people, the job can offer the challenge of a constant flow of changing faces to be helped through the flight.

Some airlines that rely mainly on summer tours recruit on a short-term seasonal basis. Other companies do employ part-time staff who often tend to cover short-haul routes.

The airlines tend to set their own standards for recruitment, often looking for a good general education and some experience of dealing with the public. Most of the airlines ask for a good working knowledge – or better – of at least one foreign language and many have restrictions on the minimum and maximum height and weight.

⭐ *Air cabin crew must have a smart appearance and a friendly manner.*

Minimum requirements for flight attendants

- The minimum age is usually 20 years or more.
- Good levels of fitness and health are required, including good eyesight – although contact lenses are usually accepted.
- Height restrictions are normally between 1.57m and 1.87m (5ft 2in–6ft 2in)
- Weight needs to be 'in proportion' with height.
- Experience of dealing with the public is usually essential.
- Some companies require at least conversational ability in a foreign language.
- A good general level of education is necessary.
- Ability to swim is essential.
- All staff have to be prepared to look smart and presentable and some companies place restrictions on physical appearance – for example, disliking beards, visible tattoos and piercings.
- Staff are required to live within a 'reasonable travelling distance' of the airport where they are based.

Training

Each company tends to provide its own training, which can vary from three to six weeks. This covers the important aspects of safety procedure and customer service as well as areas like food hygiene, team working, first aid and basic survival skills.

There is usually a test at the end of the training period and this is then normally followed by a probationary period of six months with training usually being updated at regular intervals.

⭐ *Check-in staff need to remain calm and reassuring especially in a busy airport like this.*

Promotion to chief attendant or 'Number One' is possible with experience, and this role carries the responsibility of co-ordinating staff on board the plane and completing all the relevant paperwork for the flights.

Working as a flight attendant used once to be a young person's job but many airlines are now employing older staff, although it is still possible for staff to be transferred to ground duties like administration or training when they reach a certain age.

Check-in staff

Check-in staff are usually the first contact with travellers when they arrive for a flight. It is their job to register passengers, check their tickets and luggage and allocate seating arrangements on the plane.

At this point in their travels, people are often anxious and nervous about missing flights and being delayed so it is important that staff are calm and work well under pressure.

The job involves dealing with a wide variety of people and situations. It also involves handling the public and at the same time dealing with the administrative role of making sure there is no over-booking on planes, that luggage weight restrictions are followed, that all security procedures have been followed and that the plane is not likely to be delayed by late arrivals.

Seating in the plane is allocated through a computerized booking system and cabin staff are alerted to any passengers who have any particular requirements, like special diets.

What makes a good member of check-in staff?

Like those working in travel agencies, people working in airport administration have to be competent with a number of different computerized systems and a range of technology. As with flight crew, companies tend to look for people who have experience of dealing with the public and preferably some ability in a foreign language.

Many companies also look for a certain level of maturity to handle the pressures of the work and many recruit only people in their early twenties.

Applicants are attracted by the benefits of working for an airline, subsidized travel and competitive wages as well as the variety of work – and often the idea of working in an airport atmosphere.

Jan – Passenger service agent

Jan Phillips works as a passenger service agent at Heathrow Airport.

The main part of my job is usually to 'man' one of the airline's checking-in desks at Terminal Three. You have to be flexible and if the airline is short-staffed, you can find that your duties change at the last minute.

At the check-in desk I have to ensure that each passenger who travels with us has the correct ticketing for their journey. At this stage I also reserve seats on the plane for them and register if they have any special requirements like diet or access problems. It is important to make sure that each passenger's luggage is tagged and weighed. The aircraft must not be overloaded so passengers are encouraged not to bring too much luggage. It can be difficult sometimes to explain our limits, especially if there is a language problem or passengers are unused to air travel.

I always try to remember how nervous some people get when they travel. Airports can seem exciting places but to some people they are a bit overwhelming and scary. It's part of the job to try to put people at their ease. Some passengers require extra help with things like wheelchairs or buggies and we try to make time for people who have any special requirements.

A lot of our customers are travelling to India and Pakistan. For many of them English is not their first language and so it helps in my job that I have experience of several Asian languages through my own family and friends.

I started my career in travel and tourism at 16 when I left school and got a job as a trainee travel adviser in a local travel agency. I enjoyed the work and completed my training but after a few years I realized that there were opportunities for someone my age and with my background to work for the airlines. The pay and the perks of the job attracted me most initially. I now earn £26,000 per year. Airline staff and their family get to travel at very reduced rates and it means that I have seen more of the world than a lot of my friends in other jobs.

There is a downside to the job though. I have to work shifts because we operate 24 hours a day. Although we work on a rota, I don't enjoy working nights much. The job can also be very busy and pressured. We are often on the front line when it comes to customer complaints about things like aircraft delays and cancellations. It is sometimes hard to stay smiling and polite when you are facing an angry passenger at 2 a.m., but it's part of the job and you have to do it.

⭐ Airline staff aim to put travellers at their ease and make their journey as pleasant as possible.

Cruise ships and ferries

Cruise ships and ferries also offer a range of work opportunities. In the 1990s there was a revival of interest in cruise holidays and new cruise line companies were started. It is now estimated that 110,000 people are working in the cruise industry globally with almost 200 cruise ships in regular use.

There is a range of different jobs necessary to support such large operations. **Administrative work** involving sales and marketing is similar to the work of tour operators.

Large cruise ships have to offer luxury services to their customers. They are like floating luxury hotels, often sailing between cities where trips ashore are arranged. Just like hotels, customer service of a high standard is a priority.

Stewards/stewardesses

In customer service there are jobs working as **stewards/stewardesses**. The work on the sea is a little different from that in the sky. The pace is more leisurely for the passengers, but not necessarily for the staff who work there.

The work still involves waiting on the customers, but is also likely to involve cleaning and making up cabins. A certain level of maturity and experience of working with the public is sought for those wanting to work in customer service afloat.

The safety of passengers is also a priority and all staff aboard are involved in safety procedures.

Trained staff

Cruise liners also need trained people to offer specific services to their customers, such as people to work as **hairdressers**, **masseurs**, **sports instructors**, **entertainers**, **nursery nurses** and **chefs**, to name only a few.

Companies tend to recruit experienced, well-qualified staff through specialized agencies for these roles, and employ them on contract for the season. Most agencies only represent people over 23 years of age. Competition for places on the large liners can be intense although, for some jobs, the hours and conditions on board ship may be more difficult than those on dry land.

The purser's department

The purser's department on a cruise ship and ferry is the centre of customer services on board. A **purser** is like a hotel manager whose job it is to make sure that passengers enjoy their trip and have everything that they require.

Both clerical and organizational skills are needed for the work as well as patience and good communication skills. Once again it helps to have knowledge of a foreign language. People tend to enter the job with experience in hotel and catering.

Because of the nature of the work and the need for all staff on board, whatever their role, to have responsibility for safety at sea, shipping companies only employ people in their early twenties or older.

Working on cruise liners means living and working in close contact with customers for whatever period of time the cruise lasts. Time ashore can be limited so that staff can prepare services ready for the next stage of the cruise.

Eddie – Cruise Ship Steward

Eddie Holroyd works as a steward on a liner operating cruises around the Mediterranean. He earns approximately £17,000 per year.

I have been working on various cruise ships now for several years. I started off in the hotel and catering industry after training to be a waiter when I left school. I left with only basic qualifications but wanted a job with variety and where I would be dealing with the public. I gained some qualifications as a waiter and my training gave me the experience that I needed to gain work as a steward once I was old enough to be considered. Most companies will not employ people under the age of 26 years.

Working on board ship has given me the chance to experience parts of the world that I might never have seen if I had stayed ashore. I don't get that long ashore on trips as staff take the opportunity to spruce up the liner when it is quiet. Working as a steward is a totally different way of life from working ashore. As a steward I am responsible for the smooth running of everything in the passengers' quarters. Each of us has an allocated number of passengers and we tend to work with them throughout their stay. It's important that I get to know the passengers and what they expect from the cruise as soon as possible so that we can help them to get the most out of their cruise.

The work starts even before they come on board. I work with cleaning staff to prepare cabins and as passengers arrive, it is my job to carry their luggage to their cabins and make sure that they are settled in well. On smaller liners stewards have to do a variety of duties – working in accommodation and in the dining areas. On the larger cruise liners it is possible to specialize, and in my present job I am now the assistant supervisor responsible for all accommodation services.

The main hardship of the job is the time that you have to spend away from friends and family ashore. There is also an element of insecurity because many contracts are short term and you have to be aware of where the next opportunity might arrive. There is a number of agencies that exist to recruit for cruise line employers.

It is important for a steward to be aware of what else is happening on-board ship. Passengers expect you to be an oracle on everything on-board, from what entertainment is available to the best choices on the wine list!

⭐ This is the full crew of a cruise liner.

Getting into travel and tourism

There is such a huge variety of work covered by the loose title of 'work in travel and tourism' that it is difficult to describe ways of getting into the industry without being more specific about each job. There are, however, ways that you can prepare for many jobs in the industry as well as certain characteristics that are useful and this chapter takes you through some of them.

Many of your career decisions will depend on what you as an individual want to do next and to an extent, what sort of job you are heading for. Whether you want to stay on in education after your GCSEs or whether you want to begin your training in employment – the decision has to be yours.

Pre-16 options

Some schools may offer Foundation or Part One GNVQs in Travel and Tourism (and/or other related areas such as Leisure and Tourism) to pre-16-year-olds. They can be a useful basic introduction to the area and might give you some ideas about what you want to do next. However, make sure you take advice from teachers about the best course for you and don't worry if your school does not offer these courses.

Communication skills are essential for all areas, so GCSEs in subjects like English, Business Studies and History are useful. In jobs dealing with the public it helps to be confident and outgoing. Drama and Expressive Arts can help build your confidence. Being good at sport can be useful in some aspects of the industry and Geography can help give a sense of different countries and cultures. Obviously any ability with modern languages can only be an advantage.

At GCSE level you should be aiming at getting a good cross-section of subjects, choosing those that you enjoy and doing as well as you can in them. Employers and those in further and higher education are not expecting you to specialize too much at GCSE. They are more interested in a 'good general standard of education'. So, your GCSEs are over and done with. What is next?

Post-16 options

A vocational qualification in further education is a qualification that gives you training in a particular employment field.

- **General National Vocational Qualifications** in Travel and Tourism and in Leisure and Tourism are offered at different levels depending on the GCSE grades you have, how long you want to study and what you are aiming for. The courses offer practical experience and project work. Students are continually assessed and also study IT, communication and numeracy skills and usually undertake some relevant work experience.

- **Advanced GNVQ** can be taken as a full or a single award depending on what else you want to study. They can both usually be taken with AS levels or A2 levels and can be accepted for university entrance to most related courses if successful.

You might choose to continue studying more than one subject, either to spread your options because you are not ready to commit to a particular employment area or because you feel you could do well in certain subjects and want to continue them to a higher level of study, or because you enjoy them!

- **Advanced levels** (AS levels leading to full A2 levels) are available in a whole range of different subjects, including business studies and a number of languages, both of which are useful subjects for the travel and tourism industry. It is important that you have achieved certain grades at GCSE to ensure success. You are likely to study for two years taking up to five subjects to AS level at the end of the first year, then dropping to three or four subjects to follow up to the full A2 level. Remember you can mix and match A, AS and Advanced GNVQ full and single qualifications. You are also likely to study key skills including IT, communication and numeracy skills.

Experienced staff help new recruits to learn the trade.

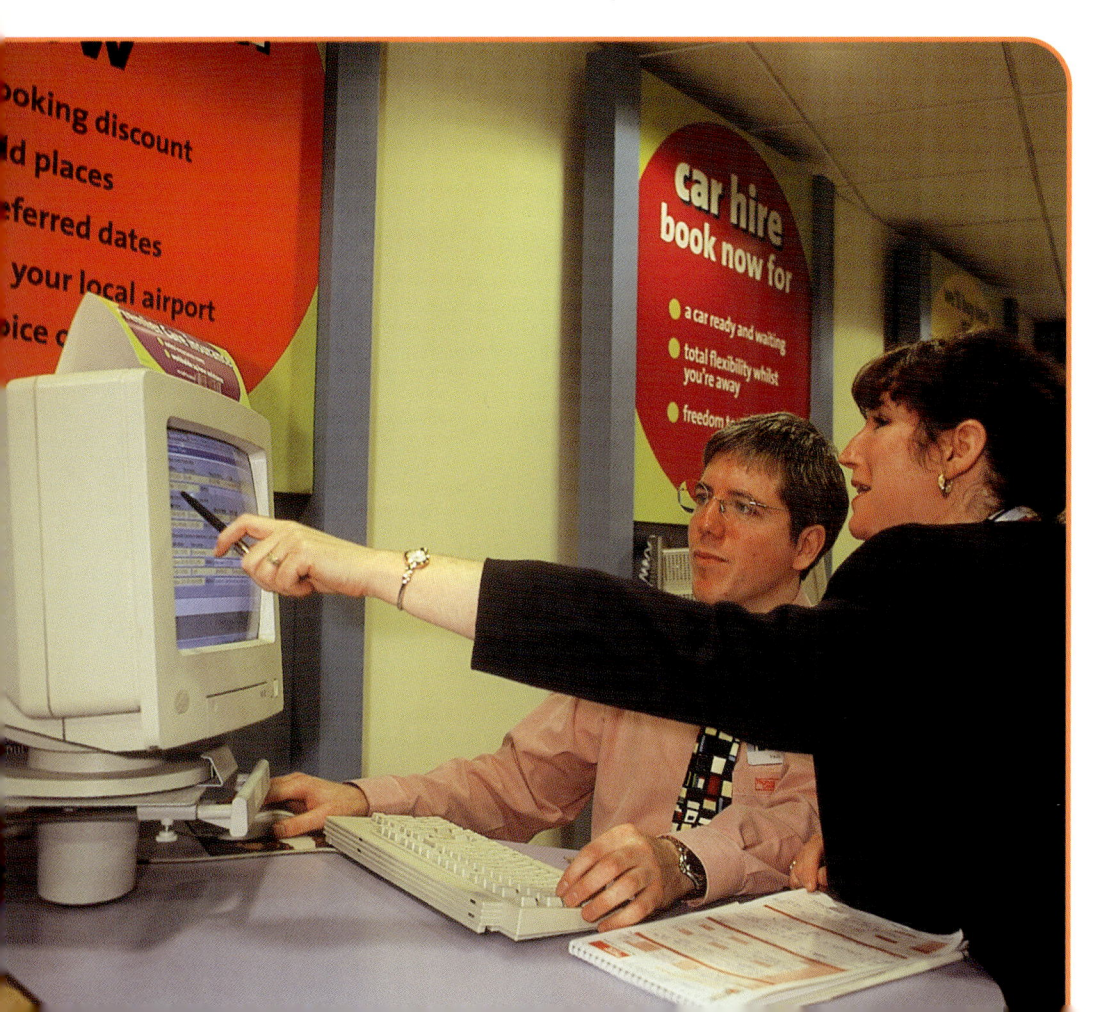

- **National Vocational Qualifications** (NVQs) at levels 2 and 3 in Travel Services are offered by the Travel Training Company. They train young people who are employed by travel agencies and tour operators. Training is mainly carried out at work and assessed by an approved trainer. It is possible to enter Higher Education courses with the right level of NVQs.

- **Higher National Diplomas/Higher National Certificates** are offered in a number of travel and tourism related subjects in many colleges and universities. HNDs are normally studied full time over two years. HNCs are offered as equivalent part-time courses usually over a longer period of time. Entry to HND/C is usually through A levels, Advanced GNVQ, Advanced NVQ qualifications or equivalents.

- **Degrees** in travel and tourism related subjects are available in universities across the country for those with appropriate further education qualifications.

  Degrees in Languages and/or Business Studies can be useful for entry to the industry. It is possible to take Travel and Tourism alongside a number of other useful subjects including IT, Public Relations, Advertising and Marketing.

  Sandwich degrees, where a period of time is spent working in a relevant area, are popular with students and employers. These are particularly useful in an industry where experience of dealing with the public is essential.

  Degree courses usually last three or four years and can sometimes be taken part time.

⭐ *Courses in travel and tourism related subjects are available in universities across the country.*

It is becoming increasingly common for people applying for higher education courses to consider a gap year. This time between school and college or university can be spent working, studying or travelling. There is a wide range of opportunities to spend arranged time in other countries outside the UK working in education, Camp America or experiencing other cultures. As we have seen, many tour operators offer short-term contracts as resort rep or holiday couriers to people wanting to gain experience of dealing with the public.

Useful information, addresses & contacts

If you are interested in a career in travel and tourism, or think you might be, there are many things that you can do to find out more.

You should be able to find lots of information in your school careers library or the library of your local Careers Service. You will find travel and tourism information under GAX in the library catalogue.

For information about NVQs, National Traineeships and Modern Apprenticeships ask your careers adviser or careers teacher for opportunities in your local area.

⭐ Surfing the net can be a good way to find information about jobs in travel and tourism.

TRAVEL & TOURISM

Help yourself

Any opportunity that you get to talk to people actually working in travel and tourism, take it!

Work experience

If your school offers work experience then ask about opportunities with local employers offering travel and tourism services. You might not learn how to book around-the-world cruises in one week, but there may well be things that you can do and it will give you a real insight into the industry. And if there is no direct travel and tourism experience available remember that it is a 'people' job – any experience of dealing with the public will be useful.

CONSIDER THIS...

THE NEXT TIME YOU TRAVEL OR GO ON HOLIDAY MAKE SURE YOU FIND OUT AS MUCH AS POSSIBLE ABOUT THE ROLES OF THE PEOPLE WHO WORK TO GET YOU THERE AND KEEP YOU HAPPY!

DON'T BE SHY – MOST PEOPLE LOVE THE CHANCE TO TALK ABOUT THEMSELVES AND THEIR WORK!

The following organizations will each give you more information on travel and tourism careers.

Association of British Travel Agents
68-71 Newman Street
London
W1P 4AH
Tel: 020 7637 2444
Fax: 020 7637 0713
www.abtanet.com

Association of Independent Tour Operators (AITO)
133a St Margaret's Road
Twickenham
Middlesex
TW1 1RG
Tel: 020 8744 9280

English Tourist Board/British Tourist Authority
Thames Tower
Black's Road
London
W6 9EL
Tel: 020 8846 9000
Fax: 020 8563 0302
www.visitbritain.com

Guild of Registered Tour Guides
The Guild House
52d Borough High Street
London
SE1 1XN
Tel: 020 7403 1115
Fax: 020 7378 1705
www.bluebadge.org.uk-guild

The Travel Training Company
The Cornerstone
The Broadway
Woking
Surrey
GU21 5AR
Tel: 01483 727321
Fax: 01483 756698
www.abtanet.com

Institute of Travel and Tourism
113 Victoria Street
St Albans
Hertfordshire
AL1 3TJ
Tel: 01727 854395
Email: itta@dial.pipex.com

The National Training Organization for Sport, Recreation and Allied Occupations
24 Stephenson Way
London
NW1 2HD
Tel: 020 7388 7755
Fax: 020 7388 9733
www.spirito.org.uk

British Airports Authority
First Point
Buckingham Gate
Gatwick
West Sussex
RH6 OH2
www.baa.co.uk

UCAS
Rosehill
New Barn Lane
Cheltenham
Gloucestershire
GL52 3LZ
Tel: 01242 222444
www.ucas.co.uk

Other publications

Working in Tourism and Leisure, published by COIC (Central Office for Information on Careers)

Careers in the Travel Industry, published by Kogan Page

Jobs in Travel and Tourism, published by Kogan Page

Working in Travel, ABTA guide published by The Travel Training Company

Working on Cruise Ships, published by How to Books.

Travel trade newspapers can be a useful source of information. Vacancies can be found for a whole range of travel and tourism jobs. Look for *Overseas Job Express*, *Travel Trade Gazette* and *Travel Weekly* at your local library, or surf the net for their websites.

> **CONSIDER THIS...**
> SOME MAJOR EMPLOYERS HAVE THEIR OWN WEBSITES OUTLINING TRAINING AND JOB OPPORTUNITIES THAT THEY OFFER, FOR EXAMPLE, BRITISH AIRWAYS: WWW.BRITISHAIRWAYS.COM

Also look at the web

Have a look around the web to see what you can find:

Career Compass, at www.ttjobs.com

gives you a lot of basic information on jobs, as well as the chance to access other sites for connected career ideas.

Getting started in the cruise entertainment industry at www.jcoston.bizland.com

and *A guide to jobs and careers at sea* at www.matandmore.ndirect.co.uk

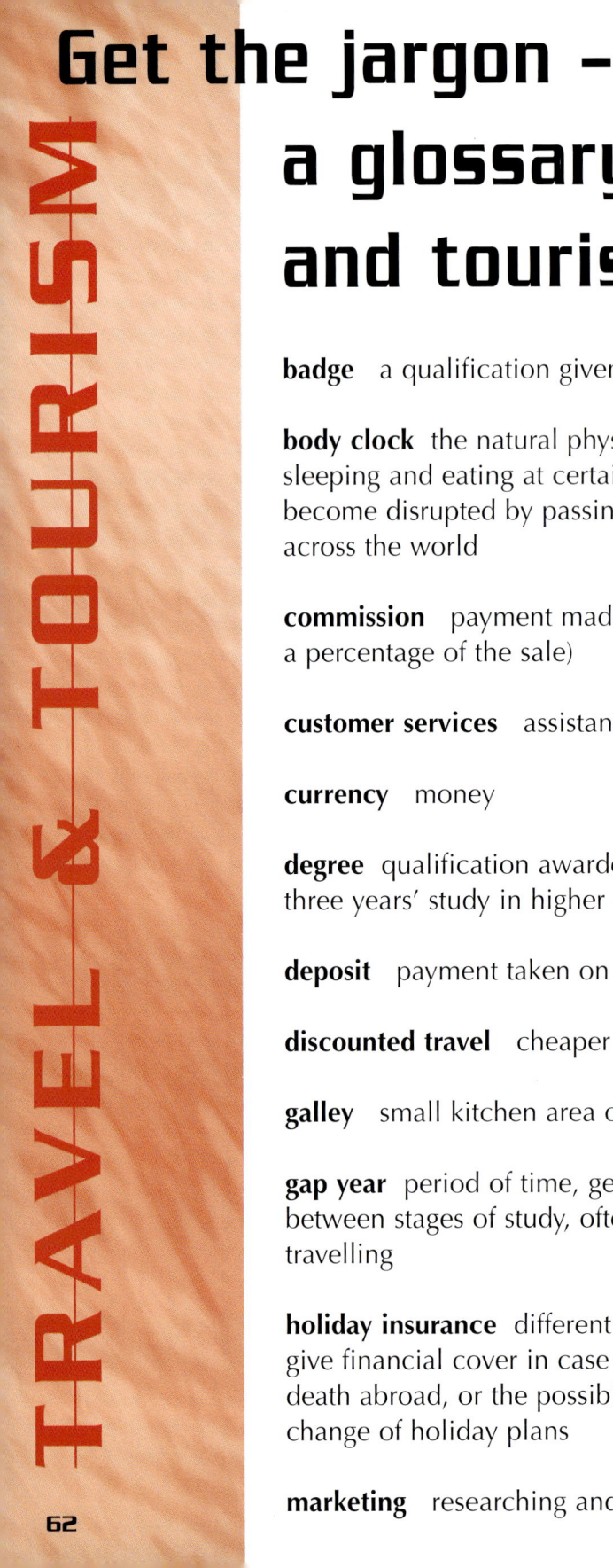

Get the jargon – a glossary of travel and tourism terms

badge   a qualification given to tourist guides

body clock   the natural physical cycle of the body, like sleeping and eating at certain times, which can become disrupted by passing through time zones across the world

commission   payment made for securing sale (usually a percentage of the sale)

customer services   assistance given to customers

currency   money

degree   qualification awarded usually after two or three years' study in higher education

deposit   payment taken on booking to reserve holiday

discounted travel   cheaper than usual prices for travel

galley   small kitchen area on a ship or plane

gap year   period of time, generally 12 months, between stages of study, often spent working or travelling

holiday insurance   different types of insurance which give financial cover in case of accident, illness or death abroad, or the possibility of cancellation or change of holiday plans

marketing   researching and promoting sales

operations the day-to-day working business of a company

package holiday the putting together of the key items of a holiday (travel, accommodation and insurance) to make one 'product' to be purchased by the holidaymaker

product knowledge understanding of what is being offered for sale

promotions special events to push something forward for sale

public relations working for good company profile in the press and media

retailing selling products and services direct to customers

sandwich degrees where a significant time is spent in related employment throughout the course of a degree

service industry the supply of services – catering, accommodation, retail, travel, entertainment – to the public as opposed to the supply of manufactured goods or products; one of the largest growth industries in the world

short haul flight one- or two-hour plane journey

super services areas of work said to be likely to dominate employment in the future

tourist information centre organization that promotes an area to tourists and provides a service for giving information and answering queries

traveller's cheques method of payment when travelling abroad

Index

airline staff 7, 8, 39–47
airline steward/stewardess 40–4
A levels 54

business travel 14

chalet maid 20
check-in staff 44–5
chef 49
children's rep 23, 24
courier 7, 22–7
courses and qualifications 53–5
cruise ships and ferries 48–51
customer services 8, 18
customers 6

degrees 55

entertainment staff 25, 49

flight attendant 7, 8, 40–4

GCSEs 52–4
General National Vocational Qualifications (GNVQs) 12, 52–5

hairdresser 49

IT skills 11, 14, 15, 21

language skills 25, 29, 30, 38, 42, 45

marketing staff 19, 21
masseur 49

National Vocational Qualifications (NVQs) 12, 15, 55
nursery nurse 49

package holidays 9, 14, 16–17, 20, 25
passenger service agent 46–7
pay and conditions 8, 13, 26, 28, 33, 36, 46, 50
purser 49

reservations staff 18
resort representative 16, 22–7

sales staff 19, 21
self employment and part-time work 21, 31, 42
school subjects 52–3
short-term contracts 7, 21, 23, 42, 50, 56
ski holidays 20
skills and qualities required 8, 11, 15, 18, 21, 25, 30, 33, 38, 43, 45, 49
sports instructor 49

tour contractor 20
tourist information assistant 34, 35, 36–8
tourist information centres 34–5
training 15
travel agent 8, 10–15

work experience 58